2/14/07 DAVIDSON $20.95 YANF

The Library of Sexual Health™

CHLAMYDIA

AMY BREGUET

The Rosen Publishing Group, Inc., New York

For Charlie

Published in 2007 by The Rosen Publishing Group, Inc.
29 East 21st Street, New York, NY 10010

Library of Congress Cataloging-in-Publication Data

Breguet, Amy.
Chlamydia/by Amy Breguet.
   p. cm.—(The library of sexual health)
Includes bibliographical references.
ISBN-13: 978-1-4042-0909-1
ISBN-10: 1-4042-0909-3 (library binding)
1. Chlamydia trachomatis—Juvenile literature. I. Title. II. Series.
QR82.C35B74 2006
616.95'18—dc22

                                                        2006004012

Manufactured in the United States of America

CONTENTS

INTRODUCTION

Sexually transmitted diseases (STDs) are more common than many people might think—and not just among adults. In fact, according to the Centers for Disease Control and Prevention (CDC), 19 million new STD infections occur each year. Almost half of them are among young people between the ages of fifteen and twenty-four.

Chlamydia remains the most frequently reported bacterial STD in the United States. In 2004, more than 900,000 cases were reported, and the case rate for females was 3.3 times higher than it was for males. However, since most people with the disease are not even aware of their infection—and therefore do not seek testing—this figure is much lower than the actual number of chlamydia cases.

It is estimated that nearly three million Americans are infected annually. A disproportionate number of these are adolescent girls.

Chlamydia is caused by bacteria called *Chlamydia trachomatis*. Like other STDs, it is spread through sexual contact. This doesn't mean vaginal intercourse only. A person can get chlamydia if he or she has oral or anal sex with an infected partner, too.

Because it often has no symptoms, chlamydia is sometimes known as a "silent" disease. In some cases, symptoms never appear, even as the disease progresses and causes serious damage to a person's reproductive system. If severe enough, this damage can make it difficult for female sufferers to have children. Since chlamydia can cause problems if left untreated, anyone who is sexually active should learn about testing and treatment.

The good news is there are simple tests that can detect chlamydia, even when there are no symptoms. Your doctor or a clinic can perform these tests. Once the disease is diagnosed, chlamydia can be treated easily with antibiotics (drugs that kill bacteria).

Chlamydia, like all other STDs, is preventable. The one and only sure way to avoid STDs is to not have oral, anal, or vaginal sex. If you do choose to have sex, latex condoms (when used correctly and all the time) are highly effective in preventing the spread of STDs.

In a world of mixed messages, it's not always easy to do the "right" thing. Media—such as TV, movies, and the

Internet—can strongly influence how you think and behave. Studies show that what young people watch can particularly affect their attitudes about relationships and sex. This finding is of concern, considering the serious lack of references to STDs in TV storylines. In real life, the consequences from having unprotected sex, such as pregnancy and contracting STDs, are far from rare.

You might be hesitant to discuss sex and STDs with a health-care provider. Although it can be awkward at first, these professionals are trained to listen and take your

Learning about STDs, as this high school class is doing, is the first step toward preventing them.

concerns seriously. It is never a mistake to bring up something that is worrying you. It could be a much bigger mistake if you keep it to yourself.

Sexual health is an area of your life where you can be in control. It all comes down to making smart choices. This book can help.

CHAPTER ONE

What Is Chlamydia?

Chlamydia is a common bacterial STD. In fact, it continues to be the most frequently reported STD in the United States, year after year. Some sources indicate that this reflects its prevalence throughout world history. As stated in *The Microbial Biorealm*, a 2004 report from Kenyon University's biology department, chlamydia "has long plagued humanity as the most commonly contracted STD."

Chlamydia trachomatis, the bacteria that causes the STD, is one of three species of the family of bacteria called *Chlamydiaceae*. *Chlamydia trachomatis* can also cause other infections, such as conjunctivitis (an eye infection) and pneumonia. Other species include *Chlamydia pneumoniae* (which can cause pneumonia, sinusitis, and bronchitis) and *Chlamydia psittaci* (which is carried by birds). But unless you are in medical school, "chlamydia" generally refers to the STD.

Identified in 1907, chlamydia was once thought to be a virus (a kind of germ that cannot easily be treated with drugs). It was classified as a bacterium in the 1960s, when it was found to make its own proteins and have other characteristics of bacteria. The word "chlamydia" comes from the Greek root *chlamys*, a type of cloak that drapes over the shoulder. This refers to the way the chlamydia bacterium drapes itself around the nucleus of cells it attacks. It multiplies within the cell, then exits and moves on to other cells.

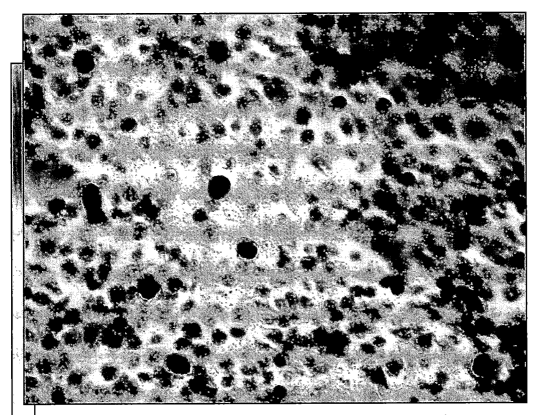

The *Chlamydia trachomatis* bacterium seen here has been magnified fifty times under a microscope.

WHO GETS CHLAMYDIA?

Chlamydia and other STDs are not spread through casual contact. This means you can't get chlamydia from a doorknob or toilet seat, or from shaking hands, hugging, or hanging out with someone who has it. It also is not spread through kissing. Chlamydia can affect anyone who has sexual contact with an infected person. In the United States, the highest rates of the STD occur among young women in their teens and twenties, and rates are higher among African Americans. Although about three million new cases appear in the United States each year, tens of millions more occur worldwide.

One reason young women are at such high risk for chlamydia is the fact that the cervix, the opening of the uterus (where a baby grows), of an adolescent girl is not fully developed. If the bacteria enters the body through her vagina, the underdeveloped cervix makes a better environment than a grown woman's cervix for the bacteria to thrive. Young people may also be at higher risk because they are still developing their decision-making skills about sex and sexual activity.

HOW IS CHLAMYDIA SPREAD?

Chlamydia bacteria live in an infected woman's vaginal secretions or in an infected man's semen (fluid that carries sperm). This means that if someone has chlamydia, he or she can pass it to someone else during vaginal, anal, or

Ten Facts About Chlamydia

1. Chlamydia is the most commonly reported bacterial STD in the United States.

2. Chlamydia is the most common STD among teens.

3. Adolescent girls are much more likely than adult women to contract chlamydia and to contract it more than once.

4. Many people who have chlamydia also have gonorrhea, another common bacterial STD.

5. Chlamydia can invade cells without actually damaging them, leaving the victim symptomless.

6. Pelvic inflammatory disease (PID), usually caused by untreated chlamydia or gonorrhea, is a leading cause of infertility (inability to have a baby) in women.

7. Women with chlamydia are up to five times more likely to contract HIV, the virus that causes AIDS, if they are exposed to it.

8. In areas of the world plagued by poverty and overcrowding, seven to nine million people become blind due to chlamydial infection.

9. Chlamydial infections are responsible for $3 billion to $4 billion in health-care costs each year. With complications included, the figure rises to about $24 billion.

10. Chlamydia is 100 percent preventable.

oral sex. The greater the number of sexual partners a person has, the greater the risk of contracting chlamydia. A pregnant woman can also pass chlamydia to her baby during birth, which can cause a number of health problems for the baby.

Depending on how it was spread, the germ may invade the cervix, vagina, penis, rectum (the canal that connects the colon and anus), urethra (the tube that carries urine), or throat. In addition, it can travel from hand to eye, causing conjunctivitis (an eye infection also called pinkeye). In the United States, infection of the throat and eye is less common than infection of sexual organs. In impoverished regions, however, where crowding and unsanitary conditions are a problem, chlamydial eye infections are common. In parts of Africa and the

A farmer in Vietnam is examined at a local medical center for trachoma, an inflammatory eye condition caused by chlamydia. Vietnam hopes to eliminate the disease by 2010.

Middle East, for example, chlamydia is often spread not only through sexual contact, but through infected people's eye secretions. People with chlamydial eye infections can suffer from trachoma, a chronic inflammatory condition that can lead to blindness. It is estimated that worldwide, seven to nine million people are blind due to chlamydial infection.

What Are the Symptoms?

Because of the way chlamydia operates, it is able to cause infection without actually damaging cells. This is why more often than not, a person with chlamydia shows no symptoms. The person may have no idea that he or she has the disease until a test proves it. This is especially true for women—fewer than 30 percent of those infected show symptoms.

If there are symptoms, they usually appear one to three weeks after sexual contact with an infected person. They may be mild and only last a short time. In women, symptoms include:

- Increased or abnormal vaginal discharge
- Pain or a burning feeling when urinating
- Irritation or itching around the vagina
- Bleeding after sexual intercourse or other abnormal vaginal bleeding
- Pain in the lower abdomen or lower back, nausea, or fever, if the infection has spread to the uterus or

fallopian tubes (where eggs move from the ovaries to the uterus)

Among infected men, symptoms are slightly more common and may include:

- A clear, white, or yellowish discharge from the penis
- A burning feeling when urinating
- Burning or itching around the opening of the penis
- Pain or swelling of the testicles

If chlamydia is spread through anal sex, rectal symptoms may appear. For both men and women, these include pain, discharge, and bleeding. The appearance of one or more possible symptoms of chlamydia warrants a doctor's visit.

CHAPTER TWO

Silent Damage: Complications of Chlamydia

I f chlamydia symptoms are so mild—when they're present at all—then why be concerned? In fact, that's exactly the reason for concern. The lack of symptoms, ironically, is what can make the disease dangerous. Untreated chlamydia can lead to some serious problems, particularly for women.

The main problem with chlamydia isn't the localized infection. It is the effects the disease can have if it is allowed to continue living within the body. Unfortunately, this happens more often than people realize since they are often unaware they're infected. Over months or even years, the disease can quietly wreak havoc on a person's reproductive system.

PELVIC INFLAMMATORY DISEASE: A HOST OF PROBLEMS FOR WOMEN

Each year in the United States, more than one million women experience an episode of pelvic inflammatory disease (PID). PID most often results from an untreated bacterial STD. In fact, up to 40 percent of women with untreated chlamydia develop PID. STD-related PID occurs when the disease spreads from the initial site of infection to internal reproductive organs—the cervix (which is the infection site in many cases), uterus, fallopian tubes, or ovaries. Because of the multiple problems it can cause, PID is the single most devastating complication of chlamydia.

Since young women are at such high risk for chlamydia, it is not surprising that this group also has the highest rate of PID. Having multiple sex partners and/or not using

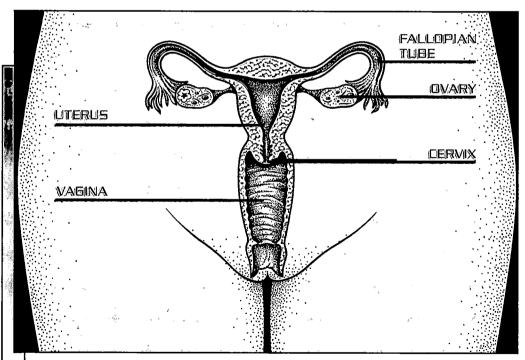

Pelvic inflammatory disease (PID) can cause serious damage to a woman's reproductive organs, including the fallopian tubes, ovaries, uterus, cervix, and vagina.

condoms when having sex may put young women more at risk for PID.

What Are the Symptoms of PID?

When caused by chlamydial infection, PID often has no noticeable symptoms. If symptoms do occur, they are usually mild and vague. (On the other hand, when PID is caused by gonorrhea, symptoms may be severe.) The CDC estimates that women and health-care providers fail to recognize symptoms of PID about two-thirds of the time. Even though symptoms are absent or mild, it is still possible that severe damage is being done to the reproductive system. See your doctor if you have any of the following symptoms, especially if you are sexually active:

- Lower abdominal pain (most common symptom)
- Fever
- Unusual vaginal discharge, sometimes with an unpleasant odor
- Painful sexual intercourse
- Painful urination
- Unusual menstrual bleeding such as bleeding between periods
- Pain in the upper right abdomen

What PID Can Do

Left untreated, PID can cause permanent damage to a woman's reproductive organs. It does this by invading healthy tissue and turning it into scar tissue. Tissue scarring is the root of three major PID complications.

A particularly devastating PID-related problem is infertility, which affects about one in eight women with PID. In fact, PID is the most common and preventable cause of infertility in the United States. How does PID cause a woman to become infertile? When scar tissue forms in a woman's fallopian tubes, it can interfere with passage of sperm into the tubes to fertilize an egg. Sperm travel may be prevented, even if a tube is not totally blocked. Partial blockage or slight damage can also result in infertility.

Sometimes a sperm manages to reach and fertilize an egg, despite scar tissue. However, the scar tissue may then prevent the fertilized egg from traveling down into the uterus. The egg may implant and try to grow in the fallopian tube, possibly causing another major PID-related problem called ectopic (or tubal) pregnancy. Ectopic pregnancy causes severe pain and internal bleeding. The condition can be life-threatening if the fallopian tube bursts. Therefore, immediate surgery is often required.

PID scarring can also lead to chronic pelvic pain. This pain can last for months or even years. Some women develop PID, get treatment, and become infected again. The greater the number of times a woman has PID, the greater her chances are of becoming infertile, having an ectopic pregnancy, or developing chronic pelvic pain.

In addition to tissue-scarring-related problems, PID can cause a tubo-ovarian abscess (TOA). This is a collection of bacteria, pus, and fluid that develops in an infected woman's fallopian tube. TOA can cause fever and extreme pain—sometimes even making it difficult to walk—but can generally be cured with antibiotics and possibly surgery. Teens with PID are most likely to develop TOA.

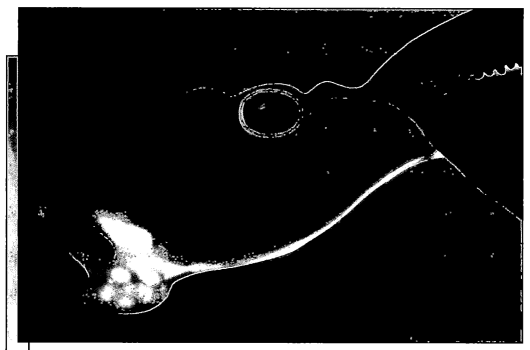

When a fertilized egg begins to grow in a fallopian tube instead of traveling to the uterus, it is called an ectopic pregnancy. This can be a life-threatening condition and often requires immediate surgery.

CHLAMYDIA AND PREGNANCY

A woman with untreated chlamydia may successfully become pregnant. But this doesn't mean she is in the clear. It means there is now another person who may be affected by complications. Most seriously, there is evidence that chlamydia can result in premature birth—a baby being born too early. A baby born prematurely often has many serious health risks due to underdeveloped body systems.

Chlamydia can cause a pregnant woman to give birth prematurely. Early birth can mean serious health problems for the baby, who may not be fully developed.

A pregnant woman with chlamydia can also pass the bacteria to her baby through childbirth. This can result in the baby's developing conjunctivitis. Symptoms of swollen eyelids and discharge from the eyes usually develop within ten days of the baby's birth. The baby could also develop pneumonia within three to six weeks of birth. Fortunately, both of these conditions can be successfully treated with antibiotics.

To prevent these complications altogether, a woman should be tested for chlamydia and other STDs as soon as she learns of her pregnancy. In general, if any test is positive, the woman should receive treatment right away.

OTHER CONCERNS FOR WOMEN

In addition to PID and problems related to pregnancy, women should be aware of a few other possible complications from chlamydia. For example, if untreated chlamydia spreads to the bladder, it can cause cystitis (a bladder infection). Cystitis symptoms include lower abdominal pain, fever, and painful urination. Chlamydia can also cause a condition called mucopurulent cervicitis, which is marked by excessive, yellow discharge from the cervix. Both conditions can be treated with antibiotics.

Many STDs, including chlamydia, make women particularly susceptible to HIV (human immunodeficiency virus), the virus that causes AIDS (acquired immunodeficiency syndrome). In fact, if exposed to the virus, a woman who has chlamydia is up to five times more likely than a chlamydia-free woman to contract HIV.

WHAT ABOUT GUYS?

Most chlamydia complications affect women. But men with untreated chlamydia have risks of their own, though the risks are somewhat rare.

Epididymitis can develop in men with chlamydia. If this happens, it means the infection has spread to the

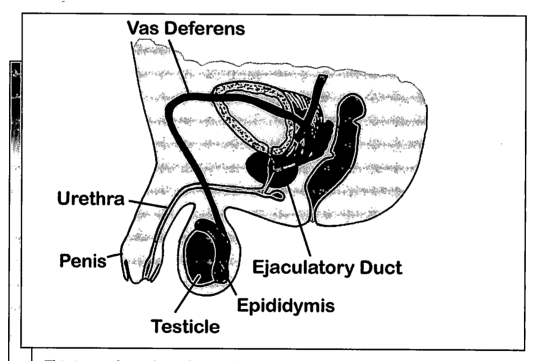

Vas Deferens

Urethra

Penis

Ejaculatory Duct

Epididymis

Testicle

This image shows the male reproductive system, which includes the penis, urethra, testicle, epididymis, ejaculatory duct, and vas deferens. Complications from chlamydia are relatively uncommon among men, but epididymitis and prostatitis can develop.

epididymis—the tube that carries sperm from the testis to the penis. Primary symptoms are pain and fever. Occasionally, epididymitis can make a man sterile (unable to produce children). Untreated chlamydia can also lead to prostatitis, an inflammation of the prostate (the gland that helps form sperm). Prostatitis symptoms can include discharge from the penis, discomfort during or after urination, discomfort during or after sex, and lower back pain. Prostatitis may also interfere with fertility. Both epididymitis and prostatitis are usually treated successfully with antibiotics.

A rare condition called Reiter's syndrome (RS) can result from chlamydia and certain other bacterial illnesses. Although RS affects both men and women, it usually strikes men between the ages of twenty and forty. Four seemingly unrelated symptoms—arthritis (joint inflammation), skin lesions, redness of the eyes, and urinary tract problems—usually characterize RS. Antibiotics and/or anti-inflammatory drugs are used to treat the disease.

This information might seem overwhelming. But, remember, complications generally happen only when chlamydia goes undiagnosed and untreated. You can avoid these worst-case scenarios by taking charge of your sexual health.

CHAPTER THREE

Testing and Treatment

I f there is any chance you may have been exposed to chlamydia, take steps to protect your health. Get tested, and, if you are diagnosed with the disease, follow treatment instructions exactly.

WHO SHOULD GET TESTED?

Everyone should see his or her health-care provider for regular checkups—especially anyone who is sexually active or considering having sex. Girls, in particular, should begin having gynecological exams once a year when they turn eighteen or become sexually active. A gynecologist, a doctor who specializes in women's health, usually performs these exams, although some general practitioners (family doctors) perform them as well.

For young women, a typical gynecologist visit involves some discussion of, and sometimes testing for, STDs. Don't assume your exam includes this—be sure to ask. A Pap test, however, is included. This routine gynecological test checks the cervix for abnormal cells that in many cases are caused

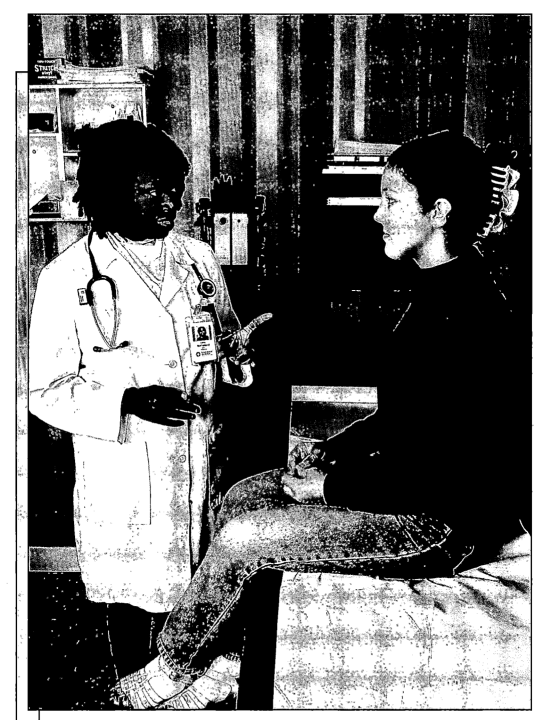

Regular doctor checkups are important—especially if you're sexually active or considering having sex. Be sure to tell your doctor if you have been experiencing any unusual symptoms.

by HPV (humanpapillomavirus), another very common STD. Medical experts recommend chlamydia testing for all sexually active women age twenty-five and under. If you are sexually active, ask your doctor about these tests.

Males who are sexually active also need to see their doctors on a regular basis. Visits should include an examination of the genitals to check for anything unusual. STD testing is also recommended for sexually active males.

Be sure to answer your doctor's questions completely and honestly, and tell him or her about anything that might be of concern. If your doctor doesn't bring up sexual

Free and low-cost clinics offer testing and treatment for STDs. Many of them offer anonymous testing.

activity or STDs, feel free to bring up the topic yourself. Your doctor is trained to listen to and answer your questions. If you have any symptoms, especially ones described in this book, be sure to tell your doctor.

If you know or suspect that a sexual partner has chlamydia, you should get tested right away. Remember that chlamydia often has no symptoms. Even if you don't notice any problems, it does not guarantee that you haven't been infected.

You do not necessarily need to see your regular doctor or gynecologist to be tested for chlamydia or other STDs. For example, you could get tested at a free or low-cost clinic, a family-planning center, or your local hospital. Some schools even offer health-care services that include testing and treatment for STDs. For information on where you can go for STD testing (or any other STD-related information), call the CDC's National STD Hotline at (800) 227-8922.

TESTS FOR CHLAMYDIA

There are several types of chlamydia tests. Some involve tissue cultures (the process of growing cells outside the body). Others look for antibodies or enzymes (types of proteins) that indicate the presence of chlamydia.

The most traditional testing method involves collecting a cell or secretion sample from the genitals. For women, this can be done easily during a gynecological exam. The health-care provider inserts a long cotton swab into the vagina to obtain a sample from the cervix. He or she may also take a sample from the rectum. For men, the health-care provider will swab the inside of the penis and/or rectum. The cell or secretion sample is sent to a lab, where technicians check for chlamydia. Results of the test are usually ready within three to seven days.

Another type of test detects chlamydia bacteria in urine. A patient provides a urine sample, which is then analyzed. This test, which has been in use since 1995, is easier and more widely accessible, especially for young people. Another advantage is that test results are usually available within twenty-four hours. Since this form of testing is still relatively new, however, it may not be available at all doctor's offices and clinics.

If a test is negative, it is unlikely you have chlamydia. Nonetheless, false results are possible with both types of tests. If you have reason to believe you might have chlamydia—especially if you know that a past or present sexual partner has it—ask to be tested

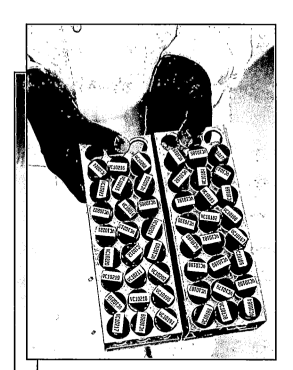

These specimen containers hold chlamydia swabs that were collected from patients at a clinic. The samples are sent to a lab and analyzed to determine if chlamydia bacteria are present.

again. Your health-care provider might recommend waiting a certain amount of time before retesting.

How Is Chlamydia Treated?

If a test comes back positive, treatment should begin immediately. Fortunately, chlamydia is easily curable. If any complications have developed, they may be more difficult to treat.

Chlamydia is treated with antibiotics, medications that kill illness-causing bacteria. Many antibiotics, including tetracycline, doxycycline, chloramphenicol, erythromycin, and amoxicillin, are used to treat chlamydia. What your health-care provider prescribes may depend on various factors, such as your age, medical history, and what you can afford. Treatment is extra critical for pregnant women who have chlamydia. During pregnancy, erythromycin and amoxicillin are the antibiotics most often prescribed.

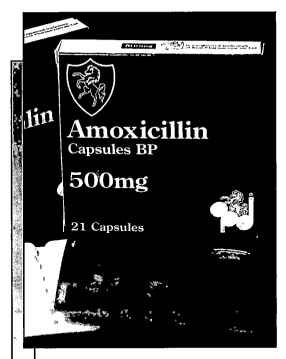

Antibiotics kill bacteria that cause illness. Amoxicillin is among the antibiotics commonly used to treat chlamydia.

An antibiotic called azithromycin may be given in one dose. While this makes treatment simple and convenient, azithromycin is significantly more expensive than other antibiotics. There may be other drawbacks, too. If you need treatment for chlamydia, ask your health-care provider which antibiotic he or she recommends and why.

TREATMENT TIPS

Once you begin treatment for chlamydia, it is important to follow your health-care provider's instructions, as well as any written directions that come with the medication. If you take the medication incorrectly or stop taking it too soon, you may kill only some of the bacteria, leaving the rest to survive and get stronger. Even if your symptoms improve, continue to take the medication until it is gone.

Anyone diagnosed with chlamydia should avoid all sexual activity until treatment is completed and successful (follow your doctor's advice on this). In some cases, such as treatment during pregnancy or when symptoms don't go away despite treatment, a health-care provider may recommend retesting for chlamydia following the course of antibiotics. If you are being treated for chlamydia and still have symptoms after finishing your antibiotics, let your health-care provider know.

TREATING PELVIC INFLAMMATORY DISEASE

Many undiagnosed or untreated cases of chlamydia develop into pelvic inflammatory disease. Since there is no specific test for PID, it is critical that sexually active young women be screened regularly for STDs. In addition, women should learn to be attuned to their bodies. Recognizing the subtle symptoms of PID and describing them accurately to a health-care provider can help make a diagnosis.

Like chlamydia, PID is treatable with antibiotics, although treatment is generally more complex than for chlamydia alone. Patients are usually prescribed at least two different antibiotics. This is because more than one type of germ may be contributing to the disease, and it's sometimes difficult to identify each one. If you are being treated for PID, as with any other treatment, follow your health-care provider's instructions exactly. He or she may ask you to return for a checkup two or three days after starting antibiotics to make sure the medicine is working.

Some women with PID need to be hospitalized. A health-care provider may recommend hospitalization if a woman with PID is very sick, is pregnant, needs IV (intravenous) antibiotics, or has an abscess in her fallopian tube or ovary. In some cases, surgery is necessary to treat PID. This can sometimes help complications such as scarring and chronic pain.

DON'T BE EMBARRASSED

Some young people might be hesitant to discuss sexual matters with a health-care provider. Remember that health-care providers are trained to listen to the needs and concerns of their patients. They understand the issues facing young people today. They aren't there to judge you—only to help protect your physical and emotional health.

It is completely understandable for you to feel embarrassed about a particular symptom, or about something you may have done. Try to remember, though, that the health-care provider has likely heard it before and is there to help you. Getting the assistance and information you need is very important.

If you have always had a parent in the room during doctor's appointments, you could tell your parent you'd prefer to go in alone. Or, ask the health-care provider if he or she could request that your parent leave the two of you alone. Even if your health-care provider is a pediatrician (a doctor for children and teens), it's still important to let him or her know you are sexually active. Answer his or her questions honestly. If you are female and have a pediatrician, he or she may refer you to a gynecologist.

Many clinics offer anonymous testing. This means that your name is not used. Instead, you are given a number or code to identify your test and results. If you want to be tested anonymously, call and check beforehand to see if it is an option.

TESTING AND TREATMENT FOR PARTNERS

If you test positive for chlamydia or any other STD, your past and present sexual partners should be tested, too. If

Ten Great Questions to Ask Your Health-Care Provider

1. How can I tell if I might have chlamydia?

2. Based on my sexual history, should I be tested for chlamydia and other STDs?

3. What is the chlamydia test like? When will I know the results?

4. If I have chlamydia, how can it be treated?

5. What are my medication instructions?

6. How much does medication cost? Will my insurance cover it?

7. What can happen if the disease isn't treated?

8. Will you need to tell my parents anything?

9. Do I have to tell my partner?

10. What if I have questions after I leave?

they are diagnosed with the STD, they need to begin treatment immediately. It isn't necessarily easy to tell a partner you have tested positive for an STD, but it's important. Failure to notify partners could mean helping the disease to spread.

Prevention

W hen it comes to health problems, few are more preventable than sexually transmitted diseases. Even if you decide to have sex, there are ways you can protect your health—and your partner's.

ABSTINENCE: THE FIRST LINE OF DEFENSE

The only sure way to avoid getting chlamydia or another STD is to not have sex. Not having sex, which is called abstinence, also guarantees unwanted pregnancy and other complicated issues that can arise from having sex. And despite what you might hear from your friends or see on television or in movies, not all young people are having sex.

Remember that anal and oral sex are also sex. Chlamydia and other STDs can easily spread through these activities. Abstaining only from vaginal sex may prevent pregnancy, but it won't necessarily protect you from STDs. Abstinence means no oral, anal, or vaginal sex. Since abstinence and "virginity" mean different things to different people, it is very important to talk to any partners about what abstinence or virginity means to them. Communication is key. If your partner is engaging in unprotected sex of any kind, he or she may have put him- or herself at risk for STD transmission, in turn putting you at risk.

Even if you have a boyfriend or girlfriend and are in love, it doesn't necessarily mean you are ready to have sex. There are many things to think about when making this decision. Besides the physical risks, having sex could have other effects on your life. Sex can be emotional territory. When emotions are high, so is the possibility of getting hurt. For example, breaking up—if it happens—may be that much more difficult if you have had sex. A relationship made more intense by sexual activity can also make you lose your focus on other important things in life—like friendships and activities that are critical to your future.

CONDOMS: CRITICAL PROTECTION

If you decide to have sex, there is no way to be 100 percent sure you are having safe sex. The best way to protect yourself and your partner, however, is to use a latex condom. Latex condoms are highly effective against STDs—but only if you use them correctly, every single time you have any kind of sex. Condoms are the one form of birth control that also protects against STDs. Other types of birth control, such as diaphragms or contraceptive pills or patches, only help prevent pregnancy. This means that even if you are using another form of birth control, you still need to use condoms. (People who are allergic to latex can use polyurethane condoms, although these may not protect against STDs as well as latex ones. Lambskin condoms are not recommended for STD protection, as some STDs can pass through them.)

Knowing how to use a condom correctly is important. It may seem like a no-brainer, but it's not hard to make mistakes with condoms. Here are some things to keep in mind:

Condoms, if used correctly, are the only type of birth control that helps protect against STDs.

- Always check the expiration date on the package. Do not use expired condoms.
- Make sure the package says the condom helps protect against HIV and STDs.
- Squeeze the condom package to check for any air pockets (to make sure the package is sealed). If the condom or its wrapper appears damaged in any way, do not use the condom.
- Follow the instructions on the package. Make sure you know how to use a condom before engaging in any sexual activity.
- Put on the condom before any vaginal, anal, or oral contact. The penis must be erect before putting on a condom.
- If the condom is unlubricated, use a water-based lubricant, such as K-Y Jelly. Petroleum jelly, lotion, and other oil-based lubricants can break down latex, making the condom ineffective.
- Store condoms in a cool, dry place. Never use a condom that has been stored in a warm place such as a wallet, pocket, or glove compartment.
- Use a new condom every time. Never reuse a condom.

Insist on using (or making sure your partner uses) a condom every time you have sex. Meet any refusal with a refusal of your own: no condom, no sex. Anyone who respects you and his or her own health will agree to help make sex as safe as possible. Without a condom, you could leave yourself vulnerable to contracting chlamydia and other STDs, as well as pregnancy.

Condoms are one of the few types of birth control you can get without a prescription. They're available at many locations including drugstores, supermarkets, convenience stores, family planning clinics, and local health departments.

MONOGAMY

Before you have sex with a girlfriend or boyfriend, make sure you know each other's sexual histories. Has either of you had sex before? If you have, and you have not been tested for STDs since the last time you had sex, you should consider getting tested. Being committed won't protect you against STDs if one of you has one. If you decide to have sex, having just one partner who is STD-free is your best bet. This is called monogamy. Remember, though, monogamy is only effective if both partners are practicing it. As well as being disease-free, monogamy can also have emotional benefits. Sex may have an emotional impact. Multiply that times two or even more, and things can get complicated.

Some young people might argue that having a "friend with benefits," as long as it's understood to be monogamous, is harmless fun. Before getting into this type of relationship, realize that there may be unique risks involved. For example, since there is often no official commitment, you can't always be sure of your friend's monogamy.

SEX AND THE MEDIA

What is your favorite television show? Chances are whatever it is, it is sending some message about sex. Maybe it implies that sex is no big deal, that being in love means having sex, or that there's no real need for protection. Studies indicate that young people get more information about sexuality and relationships from the mass media than from any other source. The problem is, most of what teens are watching is fictional and doesn't reflect real life.

For example, one study found that in TV storylines, unmarried people have sex four to eight times more often

Fox's *The O.C.* is just one popular show that frequently features sexual storylines.

than married people. Another found that nearly one in ten sex scenes involves someone under age eighteen. While these portrayals may seem to imply that sex is a given in a dating relationship—especially among young people—it's not true. In fact, the percentage of teens waiting to have sex is on the rise. According to government-funded research, the number of teens abstaining from sex rose 8 percent between 1995 and 2002. Even before this increase, more teens were abstinent than were sexually active.

Perhaps most misleading of all is the lack of consequences shown on TV. Occasionally, a character may get pregnant or regret his or her decision to have sex. But these instances are rare. In 2001, the American Academy of Pediatrics' Committee on Public Education found that only 165 of the nearly 14,000 sexual references made on TV each year "will deal with birth control, self-control, abstinence, or the risk of pregnancy or STDs." It is important to remember that outside the world of television, ignoring these realities can be hazardous to your health.

PEER PRESSURE: A COMMON ROADBLOCK

You may stand firm in your beliefs and values about sex. You may feel confident in knowing how to protect yourself. Unfortunately, however, peer pressure can sometimes get in the way. Peer pressure is the influence of friends and others your age on your thoughts and actions. Sex is an area where peer pressure often comes into play. For example, someone might try to convince you to have sex with him or her, or tell you it's OK not to use a condom. Peer pressure can also be less direct. If some of your friends are having sex, for instance, you might feel like you should be, too.

Several measures can help you resist peer pressure. First and foremost, make decisions about sex before finding yourself in a relationship or sexual situation—and remind yourself why you made those decisions. They may be based on your beliefs and values, concerns for your health and future, or all of these. Keeping such thoughts in mind can help you stand firm in the face of peer pressure.

Friends can be a powerful influence. Sometimes it is easy to feel swayed by what your friends are doing and thinking. Make sure you're making decisions that you can live with.

Secondly, plan what to say before you're in "the moment." For example, you might tell your partner that respecting you means respecting your decision. You could also say that what you have is great, and you don't want to risk complicating it. Ultimately, if your partner or friend continues to do or say things that make you uncomfortable or doubt yourself, you may want to consider whether the relationship is worth holding onto.

Aside from being illegal for minors, alcohol (and drugs) can make it much harder to resist peer pressure and stick to your decisions—particularly decisions about sex. Drinking or using drugs could easily lead to doing something you might later regret. The best advice? Don't drink at all, at least for now.

SEX AND YOUR FUTURE

What do you want out of life? Maybe you dream of having a family or pursuing and succeeding in a career you love. Setting goals is actually a great way to help you make smart decisions—and stay true to them.

Some young people tend to focus on the moment, rather than thinking ahead. This is not necessarily a bad thing—enjoying today, without constantly worrying about the future, can be healthy. When it comes to sex and other risky behavior, though, a carefree moment can mean a lifetime of regret.

Consider the risk of contracting chlamydia. You could get it by having unprotected sex just one time. Because of

MYTH: You can only spread chlamydia if you have symptoms.
FACT: Many people pass chlamydia to others without knowing they have the disease.

MYTH: Only people who have multiple sex partners get chlamydia.
FACT: It can take only one sexual act with one person to contract chlamydia. Since chlamydia is far from rare, the odds of someone having it are higher than you might think.

MYTH: Chlamydia is no big deal.
FACT: Chlamydia can mean pain and discomfort, emotional upset, and if it goes undiagnosed, can result in life-altering complications.

MYTH: Once you've been treated for chlamydia, you can't get it again.
FACT: Having had chlamydia doesn't lower your risk of contracting it again. You can get chlamydia as many times as you are exposed.

its lack of symptoms, you may never know you have it—until you are married and trying to have a baby. While this scenario may seem worlds away to you, it still makes sense to give it some thought. You could also apply this thinking to other goals you may have, including short-term ones. For example, maybe you're trying to get a sports scholarship to go to college. You need to play your absolute best. The stress of an STD diagnosis or symptoms could have serious effects on your game. In short, consequences from unprotected sex can interfere with your plans for the future.

Coping with Chlamydia

Chlamydia does not have to take over a person's life. It can feel overwhelming to be diagnosed with a sexually transmitted disease. The disease can be overcome, however, both physically and emotionally.

BEYOND THE BODY: CHLAMYDIA'S EMOTIONAL IMPACT

A chlamydia diagnosis can pack more of an emotional punch than a physical one. This is largely because of the social stigma that often surrounds sexually transmitted diseases. Remember that as information and statistics have become more widely available, understanding of STDs has increased. If you have an STD, don't let shame or embarrassment keep you from moving forward with your life.

Many young people, particularly girls, who are diagnosed with an STD tend to criticize themselves for contracting the disease. A study published in the *Journal of Pediatric Adolescent Gynecology* found that girls tend to deal with an STD by focusing on self-blame rather than problem-solving. This can lead to further emotional pain and keep a person from getting treatment or talking to his or her sexual partner. If you have chlamydia and are preoccupied with self-blame, remind yourself that you took action by getting tested for the disease. This makes you a responsible person. You can use that same sense of responsibility to take steps toward being treated and protecting others.

In addition to shame or embarrassment, there are other emotions that can arise after a chlamydia diagnosis. For example, you might feel scared, confused, or betrayed.

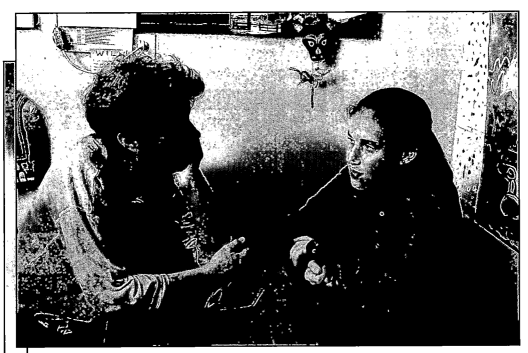

Being diagnosed with an STD can be stressful and overwhelming. It can help to talk about your feelings with someone you trust.

All of these feelings are normal and it is perfectly understandable for someone to feel this way. It can be hard to sit with them indefinitely, however. It's important to talk about your feelings with someone you trust if you feel like it could help. This might be a health-care provider, parent, other relative, clergy member, or the nurse or psychologist at your school. You can also talk to a counselor, mental health professional, or a health educator at a family planning clinic or the local health department.

Friends can be a great source of comfort in a stressful situation. Before opening up to a friend, though, you might want to be sure he or she will respect you and your privacy. While having chlamydia is no cause for shame, some people still may not understand. Remember that your sexual health issues are no one's business but yours, your health-care provider's, and your sexual partner's.

WHAT NOW?

Having emotional support in place after a chlamydia diagnosis is important. It can be the key to succeeding in the steps you need to take next.

Unlike viral STDs, such as herpes and HPV (the virus that causes genital warts), chlamydia is curable. This knowledge alone can help soften the emotional impact of the disease. Taking medication exactly as prescribed will usually cure chlamydia. But don't have any sexual contact until your health-care provider says it's OK.

TELLING A PARTNER

It is up to you to let any past or present sexual partners know about your diagnosis. The idea of telling a partner you have chlamydia is probably not appealing. You may be afraid of how he or she will react. Keep in mind that many people with STDs are pleasantly surprised at how well a partner takes the news. It's true, though, that some people might react badly, at least at first. Sometimes a person just needs time to process what it all means.

If you have been diagnosed with chlamydia, it is important to tell your partner. It might not be an easy conversation to have, but it's the right thing to do.

Sarah, age sixteen, thought you had to have sex with a lot of people to get a sexually transmitted disease. And she thought if you did get one, you'd know it—the symptoms would just be too miserable not to. She definitely had some set ideas. That was until her best friend, Julie, was diagnosed with chlamydia.

Sarah could hardly believe it when Julie called her crying. She thought it had to be a mistake. Julie was going out with Jack, her first boyfriend, and had never had sex with anyone else. In fact, Julie had only had sex with Jack a few times. He had had sex before, but only with one other person—and that was more than a year ago. Julie also said she had no symptoms at all. She had gone to the gynecologist for a checkup and her doctor had done some routine tests. The doctor had just called her with the results, telling her she had chlamydia. Both girls were completely baffled, and Julie was devastated. After all, not only did she have a sexually transmitted disease, but she assumed it meant her boyfriend must have cheated on her.

Sarah suggested that Julie come over to talk before telling Jack anything. At Sarah's house, the two friends looked up chlamydia on the Internet. Things started to make a little more sense. Many people—particularly girls and women—who have chlamydia do not have symptoms. It is also possible to have the disease for a long time, even years, and never know it. Most surprising of all was how many people get chlamydia each year—especially people their age.

Sarah told Julie she needed to tell Jack because he needed to get tested, too. She pointed out that there was a huge chance he had chlamydia and didn't know it, and that he got it before he ever started dating Julie. Julie hesitantly agreed, and the two friends spent the next hour practicing the conversation Julie would have with Jack when she went to his house that night. She promised to let Sarah know how it went.

When Julie called Sarah the next morning, she sounded much better than she had twenty-four hours earlier. The talk with Jack had gone as well as she could have hoped, and she would be going with him to the downtown health clinic after school the next day. Jack had told Julie about some weird symptoms he'd had about a year ago, but they'd been really mild and had gone away. That had been a relief, he said, because he had been too embarrassed to tell anyone. Julie told Sarah how Jack couldn't stop saying he was sorry—but that for some reason, she didn't really blame him. After all, they had both learned about chlamydia the hard way.

Sarah was sorry about what her friend went through, but it did make her rethink some things—and maybe just in time. As Julie's ordeal was ending, Sarah's relationship with her longtime crush, Tony, was just beginning.

On the other hand, you may suspect your partner passed chlamydia to you. In this case, you may feel more angry than anxious. It can be hard, but try not to make any assumptions before talking to your partner. Even if your partner does have chlamydia, he or she may have contracted it a long time ago and never had symptoms.

Talk when neither of you will be rushed for time. You may want to let your partner know ahead of time that you'd like to discuss something important, and ask him or her when a good time would be. Before any discussion, arm yourself with these tools:

- **Support.** You may want to have at least one person you can talk to before and after telling your partner. Whether you choose someone you know and trust or an objective mental health professional, it's good to have someone on your side.
- **Information.** Learn all you can about the disease so you can share those facts with your partner. He or

she will likely have questions, and it will be helpful if you have many of the answers. Stress that chlamydia is common, nothing to be ashamed of, and, above all, highly treatable.

- **Confidence.** Your purpose is to give your partner needed information—not to grovel, confess, or accuse. An excellent way to build confidence is to practice what you are going to say. You can do this in front of a mirror or role-play with your support person.

When you tell your partner(s), stress the importance of being tested. Remember that you could become infected again if you are exposed. Don't have any kind of sex with your partner until he or she tests negative or, in the case of a chlamydia diagnosis, successfully completes treatment.

HELPING A FRIEND

If a friend or family member confides in you that he or she has been diagnosed with chlamydia, he or she views you as being understanding. Consider how you would like someone to react if the situation were reversed. Try not to overreact or be judgmental. Chances are that the person is already experiencing some negative feelings. What he or she needs now is someone to be supportive. Let the person know that having chlamydia doesn't mean he or she is a bad person, and discourage the person from blaming him- or herself. Suggest keeping the focus on what to do next. For example, offer to go with the person to pick up medication or to any needed doctor's appointments.

Another way you can help is to encourage the person to tell any sexual partners, if he or she hasn't done so yet. Explain why this step is so important. Offer to help the person decide how and when to talk to partners, and even to role-play the scene. Your support could mean the difference between moving forward and hiding behind embarrassment or shame.

When going through a tough time, you might consider talking to a friend. He or she can be a good source of understanding and support.

Lastly, be trustworthy. Your friend or family member has shared some very personal information. Respect him or her by not sharing it with others.

CONTINUING TO BE CHLAMYDIA-FREE

Whether you have never been affected by chlamydia or are taking steps to deal with the disease, you can use what you have learned in this book for years to come. Remember that chlamydia is both highly curable and preventable. A disease like that should never have the chance to get the best of you—or anyone else.

GLOSSARY

abscess A cavity in the body, often filled with pus, that results from inflammation and is usually caused by bacterial infection.

anti-inflammatory Used to describe medicine that treats inflamed body tissue.

bacterial Related to germs called bacteria.

bladder The organ that holds urine until it is ready to leave the body.

colon The lowest section of the large intestine.

contract To acquire a disease.

disproportionate Notably unequal in measure to other parts of the whole.

fertilize To make capable of growing and developing.

gynecological Relating to the study and care of women's health, especially reproductive health.

impact A powerful effect.

impoverished Poor; poverty-stricken.

infertile Incapable of or unsuccessful in achieving pregnancy.

ironically In an unexpected twist; strangely.

pneumonia A disease of the lungs. Symptoms include fever, cough, chest congestion, and difficulty breathing.

prevalence The degree to which something is common or widespread.

progress To reach a more advanced stage.

relevant Important with regard to the topic at hand.

reproductive Relating to the process of creating new life.

secretions Fluids or other substances formed and released by the body.

sterile Unable to produce children or offspring.

subtle Not obvious.

thrive To grow or progress well.

American Social Health Association (ASHA)
P.O. Box 13827
Research Triangle Park, NC 27709
(919) 361-8400
Web site: http://www.ashastd.org
ASHA is one of the nation's leading authorities on sexual health. Its Web site offers a wide range of information on chlamydia and other STDs.

Canadian Federation for Sexual Health (CFSH)
1 Nicholas Street, Suite 430
Ottawa, ON K1N 7B7
Canada
(613) 241-4474
Web site: http://www.ppfc.ca
A member of the International Planned Parenthood Federation, CFSH works to promote healthy sexuality throughout Canada.

Centers for Disease Control and Prevention (CDC)
1600 Clifton Road
Atlanta, GA 30333
(800) 232-4636 (STD Hotline)

Web site: http://www.cdc.gov/node.do/id/0900f3ec80009a98
Part of the U.S. Department of Health and Human
Services, the Centers for Disease Control and Prevention is
a leading infectious diseases organization. Its STD hotline
offers a wealth of information, as well as referrals to
health-care services.

Planned Parenthood Federation of America
434 West 33rd Street
New York, NY 10001
(800) 230-PLAN (230-7526)
Web site: http://www.plannedparenthood.org
Planned Parenthood has long provided information on a
range of issues relating to sexual health and responsibility.
You can find Planned Parenthood's health centers, which
are located throughout the United States, by contacting
the organization.

The Sexuality Information and Education Council of the
     United States (SIECUS)
130 West 42nd Street, Suite 350
New York, NY 10036-7802
(212) 819-9770
Web site: http://www.siecus.org
SIECUS provides information, education, and services to
the public on matters relating to sexuality, including
sexual health.

WEB SITES

Due to the changing nature of Internet links, the Rosen Publishing Group, Inc., has developed an online list of Web sites related to the subject of this book. This site is updated regularly. Please use this link to access the list:

http://www.rosenlinks.com/lsh/chla

FOR FURTHER READING

Bell, Ruth. *Changing Bodies, Changing Lives*, 3rd ed. New York, NY: Three Rivers Press, 1998.

Daugirdas, John T. *STD: Sexually Transmitted Diseases*, 2nd ed. Hinsdale, IL: MedText, 1992.

Hatchell, Deborah. *What Smart Teenagers Know . . . About Dating, Relationships, and Sex*. Santa Barbara, CA: Piper Books, 2003.

McCoy, Kathy, and Charles Wibbelsman. *The New Teenage Body Book*. New York, NY: Perigee Books, 1998.

Stanley, Deborah A., ed. *Sexual Health Information for Teens: Health Tips about Sexual Development, Human Reproduction, and Sexually Transmitted Diseases* (Teen Health Series). Detroit, MI: Omnigraphics, 2003.

Thacker, John, Rachel Kranz, and Michael Brodman. *Straight Talk About Sexually Transmitted Diseases*. New York, NY: Facts on File, 1993.

BIBLIOGRAPHY

American Social Health Association. "Emotional Issues: Coping in a Relationship." Retrieved January 30, 2006 (http://www.ashastd.org/herpes/herpes_emotional_relationship.cfm).

American Social Health Association. "STD Prevention Partnership Position Statement: Adolescents and Sexually Transmitted Diseases." Retrieved January 10, 2006 (http://www.ashastd.org/involve/involve_adv_adolpos.cfm).

Baker, J.G., et al. "Adolescent Girls' Coping with an STD: Not Enough Problem Solving and Too Much Self-Blame." *Journal of Pediatric and Adolescent Gynecology*, May 2001, Vol. 14, No. 2.

Barth, Werner F., and Kinim Segal. "Reactive Arthritis (Reiter's Syndrome)." *American Family Physician*, August 1999, Vol. 60, No. 2.

Cates, J. R., N. L. Herndon, S. L. Schulz, and J. E. Darroch. *Our Voices, Our Lives, Our Futures: Youth and Sexually Transmitted Diseases*. Chapel Hill, NC: School of Journalism and Mass Communication, University of North Carolina at Chapel Hill, 2004.

CBS News Healthwatch. "Study: Fewer Teens Having Sex." 2004. Retrieved January 30, 2006 (http://

www.cbsnews.com/stories/2004/12/10/health/main660445.shtml).

Centers for Disease Control and Prevention. "Chlamydia." 2004. Retrieved January 10, 2006 (http://www.cdc.gov/std/chlamydia/stdfact-chlamydia.htm).

Damon-Moore, Laura, et al. "The Microbial Biorealm: A Microbial Diversity Resource." Kenyon University. 2004. Retrieved January 12, 2006 (http://biology.kenyon.edu/Microbial_Biorealm/index.html).

DeMets, Andrea. "Chlamydia trachomatis." University of Wisconsin-Madison Department of Bacteriology. 1998. Retrieved January 12, 2006 (http://www.bact.wisc.edu/Bact330/lecturechlamydia).

Guttmacher Institute. "Teen Sex and Pregnancy." 1999. Retrieved January 10, 2006 (http://www.agi-usa.org/pubs/fb_teen_sex.html).

HealthyWomen.org. "Chlamydia: Treatment." National Women's Health Resource Center. 2002. Retrieved January 30, 2006 (http://www.healthywomen.org/content.cfm?L1 = 3&L2 = 16&L3 = 2.0000).

Mayo Clinic. "Condoms: Effective Birth Control and Protection from Sexually Transmitted Diseases." 2005. Retrieved January 30, 2006 (http://www.mayoclinic.com/health/condoms/HQ00463).

Murray, Patrick R., Ken S. Rosenthal, George S. Kobayashi, and Michael A. Pfaller. "Chlamydia." Chap. 44 in *Medical Microbiology*, 3rd ed. St. Louis, MO: Mosby, 1998.

National Institute of Allergy and Infectious Disease (NIAID). "Pelvic Inflammatory Disease." 2005. Retrieved January 17, 2006 (http://www.niaid.nih.gov/factsheets/stdclam.htm).

Nemours Foundation. "Pelvic Inflammatory Disease." Retrieved January 10, 2006 (http://www.teenshealth.org/teen/sexual_health/stds/std_pid.html).

San Francisco City Clinic: Department of Public Health, City and County of San Francisco. "Chlamydia." Retrieved January 30, 2006 (http://www. dph.sf.ca.us/sfcityclinic/stdbasics/chlamydia.asp).

Shafer, Mary-Ann B., and Kathleen Tebb. "Extending Preventive Care to Pediatric Urgent Care." Presentation to STD Prevention Conference, March 10, 2004.

TeenPregnancy.org. "Teens Tell All About . . . Contraception/Birth Control." Retrieved January 12, 2006 (http://www.teenpregnancy.org/resources/teens/voices/contrace.asp).

University of California at Santa Barbara. "How to Tell Your Partner if You Have an STD." Retrieved January 30, 2006 (http://www.soc.ucsb.edu/sexinfo/?article = stds&refid = 020).

University of California at Santa Barbara. "Sexuality in the Mass Media." Retrieved January 12, 2006 (http://www. soc.ucsb.edu/sexinfo/?article = activity&refid = 026).

INDEX

ABOUT THE AUTHOR

Amy Breguet is a writer working mainly in the field of educational publishing. She has written about health, safety, and related topics in a variety of formats, many geared toward young people. She lives in Southampton, Massachusetts, with her husband and two young children.

PHOTO CREDITS

Cover, p. 4 © www.istockphoto.com/ericsphotography; cover, pp. 1, 4 (silhouette) © www.istockphoto.com/jamesbenet; pp. 1 (inset), 9 CDC/ Dr. E. Arum, Dr. N. Jacobs; p. 6 © Will Hart/Photo Edit; p. 12 © ITI Handout/Reuters/Corbis; p. 16 © John Bavosi/Photo Researchers, Inc.; p. 19 © Véronique Estiot/Photo Researchers, Inc.; p. 20 © Warren Morgan/ Corbis; p. 22 © Custom Medical Stock Photo; pp. 25, 26 © Michael Newman/Photo Edit; p. 28 © Sotiris Zafeiris/Photo Researchers, Inc.; p. 29 © Josh Sher/Photo Researchers, Inc.; p. 36 © David J. Green/Alamy; p. 39 © WB/Courtesy: Everett Collection; p. 41 © Carolyn A. McKeone/Photo Researchers, Inc.; p. 45 © Laura Dwight/Photo Edit; p. 47 © age fotostock/ SuperStock; p. 51 © www.istockphoto.com/Galina Barskaya; back cover (top to bottom) CDC/Dr. E. Arum, Dr. N. Jacobs, CDC/Dr. Edwin P. Ewing Jr., CDC/Joe Miller, CDC/Joe Miller, CDC/Dr. Edwin P. Ewing Jr., CDC.

Designer: Nelson Sá; **Editor:** Elizabeth Gavril
Photo Researcher: Marty Levick